THE WISHING TREE

For his dear friend

Victoria

on her eighth birthday

Bill he made

this Book

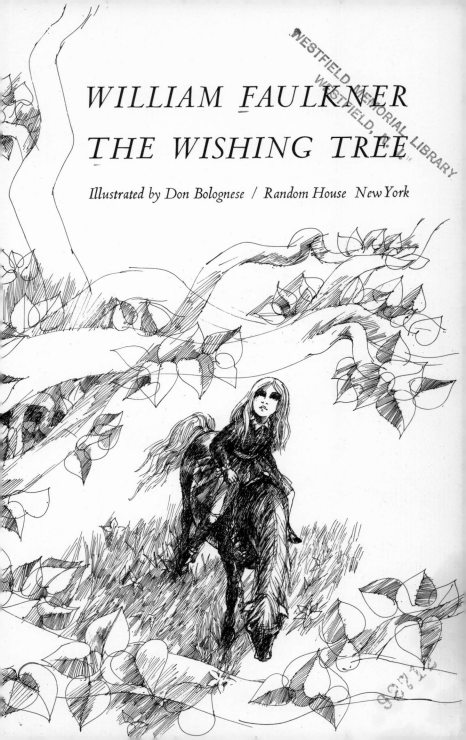

WILLIAM FAULKNER
THE WISHING TREE

Illustrated by Don Bolognese / Random House New York

To Victoria

"....... I have seen music, heard

Grave and windless bells; mine air

Hath verities of vernal leaf and bird.

Ah, let this fade: it doth and must; nor grieve,

Dream ever, thou; she ever young and fair."

THE WISHING TREE

She was still asleep, but she could feel herself rising up out of sleep, just like a balloon: it was like she was a goldfish in a round bowl of sleep, rising and rising through the warm waters of sleep to the top. And then she would be awake.

And so she was awake, but she didn't open her eyes at once. Instead, she lay quite still and warm in her bed, and it was like there was still another little balloon inside her, getting bigger and bigger and rising and rising. Soon it would be at her mouth, then it would pop out and jump right up against the ceiling. The little balloon inside her got bigger and bigger, making all her body and her arms and legs tingle, as if she had just eaten a piece of peppermint. What can it be? she wondered, keeping her eyes tight shut, trying to remember from yesterday.

"It's your birthday," a voice said near her, and her eyes flew open. There, standing beside the bed, was a strange boy, with a thin ugly face and hair so red that it made a glow in the room. He wore a black velvet suit and red stockings and shoes, and from his shoulder hung a huge empty booksatchel.

"Who are you?" she asked, looking at the redheaded boy in astonishment.

"Name's Maurice," the boy answered. His eyes had queer golden flecks in them, like sparks. "Get up."

She lay still again and looked about the room. The funniest thing was, there was nobody in the room except Maurice and herself. Every morning when she waked, her mother and Dicky would be in the room, and soon afterward Alice would come in to help her dress and get ready for school. But today there was nobody in the room except the strange redheaded boy standing beside her bed and watching her with his queer yellow-flecked eyes.

"Get up," the boy said again.

"I'm not dressed," she said.

"Yes, you are," the boy answered. "Get up."

So she threw the covers back and got out of bed, and sure enough, she was dressed—shoes and stockings, and her new lavender dress with the ribbon that matched her eyes. The red-headed boy had gone to the window and stood with his face pressed against the glass.

"Is it still raining?" she asked. "It was raining last night."

"Come and see," the boy said, and she came up beside him and saw through the window the black trees with their bare dripping branches in the rain.

"I wish it wouldn't rain, on my birthday," she said with disappointment. "I think it might stop raining today, don't you?" The redheaded boy glanced at her and then away, then he raised the window. "Oh, don't do that!" she exclaimed, then she stopped, for as soon as the window rose, instead of rain and black winter trees, she saw a soft gray mist that smelled of wistaria, and far down in the mist she heard little far voices calling, "Come down, Dulcie; Come down, Dulcie." When she looked through the upper window sash, through the glass, there was the rain, and the black sad trees, but beyond the open sash, the soft wistaria scented mist and the voices saying, "Come down, Dulcie; Come down, Dulcie."

"Well, this is the funniest thing!" she said,

looking at the redheaded boy, who was digging busily in his huge satchel.

"It's because it's your birthday," he explained.

"But nothing like this ever happened before on my birthday."

"It might have," the boy answered, taking something out of the satchel. "That's why birthdays are. And, on the night before your birthday—" he glanced at her with his queer goldflecked eyes "—if you get into bed left foot first and turn the pillow over before you go to sleep, anything might happen," he added wisely.

"Oh, that's exactly what I did last night," she said. "But who is that calling me?"

"Why not look down and see?" the boy suggested, so she leaned out the window into the warm scented mist, and there looking up at her from the ground were Alice and Dicky and George, who lived just across the street.

"Come down, Dulcie!"

"Wait for me!" she cried down to them, and

the redheaded boy was at the window again. In
his hand was a toy ladder about six inches long,
and he raised the ladder to his mouth and blew on
it, and at once the ladder began to get longer and
bigger. The redheaded boy puffed and blew, and
the ladder grew longer and longer until finally

the end of it touched the ground and Alice held
it steady while she climbed down to them.

"Got up at last, did you, Sleepyhead?"
George asked, and Dicky chanted, "Sleepyhead,
Sleepyhead!" He was a little boy, and he always
said whatever the others did.

The redheaded boy climbed down the ladder, and bent over and pressed his finger on a little shiny button on the ladder, and the air went Whishhhhhh out of the ladder and it was once more a toy ladder about six inches long. The boy put it back in his satchel. "Name's Maurice," he said shortly, looking from Alice to Dicky and then to George with his yellowflecked eyes. "Come on."

The mist was like a big tent about them and over them, and a warm little breeze blew through it, smelling of wistaria. They went across the lawn to the street, and the redheaded boy stopped again. "Well," he said, "how shall we go? walk, or in a motorcar, or on ponies?"

"Ponies! Ponies!" Dulcie and George shouted, and Dicky said, "Pony! Pony! Want to wide pony!" But Alice didn't want to.

"Naw, suh," Alice said, "me and Dicky ain't goin' to ride on no hawss, and, Dulcie, you ain't got no business with no hawss, neither."

"Oh, Alice!"

"Naw, suh," Alice repeated, "you knows your mommer don't allow you to ride no hawss."

"How do you know?" Dulcie said. "She didn't say I couldn't."

"How could she, when she don't know you's goin' to? I reckon we can get wherever we's goin' just like we is."

"Oh, Alice!" Dulcie said, and Dicky chanted, "Wide a pony, wide a pony."

"Alice and Dicky can ride in the ponycart," the redheaded boy suggested. "You aren't scared of a ponycart, are you?"

"I guess I ain't," Alice said doubtfully. "Dulcie better ride in the cart too."

"No: I want to ride a pony. Please, Alice."

"They're gentle ponies," the redheaded boy said. "Look." He reached into his satchel and brought forth a Shetland pony no larger than a squirrel, with a red bridle with little silver bells and a red saddle on it. Dulcie squealed with

delight and Dicky tried to
climb right up the boy's leg.

"Mine! Mine!" George
shouted. "First choice: I claim
first choice!"

"My pony, my pony!" Dicky
shouted. "My first choss pony!"

"Here, youall wait," the redheaded boy said,
holding the pony above his head while its little
hooves pawed and scrambled in his hand. "Stand
back, now."

So they stood back and the boy knelt and set

14

the pony on the ground, and put his mouth to the pommel of the saddle and began to blow. And as he blew, the pony got bigger and bigger stamping its feet and shaking its jingling bridle; and the boy rose to his knees and still puffed and blew, and then to his feet, and the pony got bigger and bigger. At last he raised his head.

"There," he said. "Is that big enough for you?"

"Who's that un for?" Alice asked quickly.

"Mine! Mine!" shouted George and Dicky together.

"No, this one is Dulcie's," the redheaded boy said.

"Then you let some of that air back out," Alice said promptly. "That's too big for Dulcie."

"No, no!" Dulcie objected. "Look, Alice! See how gentle he is!" She pulled up a handful of grass and the pony nibbled it and shook his head until the silver bells jingled like mad. Then she held the bridlerein and the boy took two more ponies from his satchel, and Dicky chanted, "First choss pony, first choss pony!"

"How can your satchel hold so much and yet look like it's empty?" Dulcie asked.

"Because I'm Maurice," the redheaded boy answered. "And besides, anything is likely to happen on birthdays," he added gravely.

"Oh," said Dulcie. Then the boy blew up these two ponies and gave the reins to George to hold, and took from the satchel a fourth pony hitched to a little wicker cart, with bells all over it, and Dicky was just wild. The boy blew this one up too. Alice watched nervously.

"Don't blow him up too big, now, for me and Dicky," she cautioned.

The redheaded boy puffed and blew.

"Ain't that plenty big enough?" suggested Alice uneasily.

"Alice don't want him any bigger than a rabbit," George said. "He can't pull the cart if he's not any bigger than that."

The redheaded boy puffed and blew, and soon the pony and cart were the right size. "You'll need a whip," he said, and he reached again into his satchel.

"Naw, suh," Alice said quickly, "we don't need no whip. You can put that right back."

But Dicky had already seen the whip, and when the boy put it back in the satchel, Dicky yelled. So the boy gave Dicky the whip, and Dicky and Alice got into the cart and Dicky held the end of the reins in one hand and the whip in the other.

"Drive first choss pony," Dicky shouted.

"Shetland pony, darling," Dulcie said. "Not first choice pony."

"Drive Shetland pony," Dicky said. Then Dulcie and George and the redheaded boy got on their ponies and they rode down the street.

They reached the end of the street and passed the last house, and then all of a sudden they rode out of the mist. Behind them they could see the mist like a big gray tent, but everywhere else they looked the trees were green as summer, and the grass was green and little blue and yellow flowers were everywhere. Birds were singing in the trees, and flying from one tree to another, and the sun shone and the three ponies flew along the road, faster and faster until Alice and Dicky in the cart were far behind. They stopped to wait for them, and the cart came trotting up. Alice was holding her hat on and she looked a little alarmed. So they promised not to go fast any more, and they rode on down the road and after a while they came to a small gray cottage. The cottage had roses above the door, and there was a little old man with a long gray beard sitting in the door, whittling a piece of wood.

"Good morning," the redheaded boy said politely.

"Good morning," the little old man replied politely.

"We're looking for the Wishing Tree," the redheaded boy said.

"It's a far ways," the little old man said. He shook his head gravely. "I don't believe you could find it."

"We'll ask somebody on the road," the boy said.

"There ain't anybody in these parts that ever saw it," the little old man said.

"How do you know it's so far then?" the redheaded boy asked.

"Oh, I been to it lots of times. I used to go to it every day almost, when I was your age. But I ain't been in several years, now."

"Why not come with us and show us the way?" the redheaded boy suggested. Alice was mumbling to herself and Dulcie asked,

"What did you say, Alice?"

"I says, we don't want no old trash like him with us. I bet he's a tramp. I bet your mommer wouldn't like it if she knowed."

"Come on and go with us," the redheaded boy repeated. The old man looked cautiously over his shoulder into the house.

"I believe I will," he said. He shut his knife and put it and the thing he was carving in his pocket. He rose, and peered again around the dooredge into the house. "I guess I better go and show you the way, because—"

Then the little old man's wife came to the door and threw a flatiron at him, and a rollingpin and an alarm clock.

"You lazy old scoundrel!" she shouted at him. "Sitting out here and gassing with strangers, and not a stick of wood to cook dinner with in the house!"

"Maggie," the little old man said. His wife reached into the house again and threw a shoe at him, and he turned and ran around the corner of the house. The woman stood in the door and glared at them.

"And you folks with nothing better to do than

keep folks from their work," she said. She glared at them again and slammed the door.

"There now, what I tell you?" Alice said. "White trash!"

"Well, I guess we'll have to find the Wishing Tree by ourselves," the redheaded boy said. "Come on."

They rode on past the house and along the garden fence. At the corner of the fence somebody called cautiously to them as they passed, and they saw the little old man peering out from behind a row of tomato plants.

"Is she gone?" he whispered.

"Yes," the redheaded boy answered. The little old man came out and climbed the fence.

"Wait a minute for me, and I'll go with you." So they waited for him and he sneaked along the fence to the house and picked up the clock and the rollingpin and the iron and ran back down the road and climbed the garden fence again and hid the things in the fence corner. "So she can't throw them at me when we come back," he explained cunningly.

"You can ride in the cart with Alice and Dicky," the redheaded boy said. Alice mumbled again, and Dulcie asked,

"What did you say, Alice?"

"I says, me and Dicky don't want that old trash in the cart with us. Your mommer wouldn't like it."

"Why can't I ride too?" the little old man said in a hurt tone.

"Let him ride in the cart, Alice," the redheaded boy said. "He won't bother you."

"Of course I won't, ma'am," the little old man said. "I wouldn't think of it."

"Let him ride in the cart, Alice," they all said.

"Well, get in, then," Alice said ungraciously. "But your mommer won't like it."

The little old man hopped nimbly in, and they rode on. "I can whittle things with a knife," the little old man said.

Alice sniffed.

"This is a nice pony and cart you have," the little old man said.

"First choss pony," Dicky said.

"Shetland pony, darling," Dulcie corrected. "Not first choice pony."

"I used to have a lot of ponies," the little old man said.

Alice sniffed again. "Bet you never had nothin' except flatirons throwed at you in your life."

They came to a fork in the road and the red-headed boy stopped. "Now, which way?" he asked.

"That way," the little old man answered immediately, pointing. They rode on.

"What were you carving when we came up?" Dulcie asked. The little old man reached in his pocket and took the piece of wood out, and they all crowded about the cart to look at it.

"Little puppy," Dicky said.

"It's a lizard," George said.

"No, it's a dragon," Dulcie said. "Isn't it?"

"It ain't nothin'," Alice said. "He nor nobody never saw nothin' like that."

"What is it?" Dulcie asked.

"I don't know," the little old man answered. "I don't know what it is, but I think it's a gillypus."

"What's a gillypus?" asked George.

"I don't know, but I expect it looks something like this."

"Why do you call it a gillypus, then, if you don't know what a gillypus looks like?"

"Well," the little old man answered, "it looks more like a gillypus than anything I ever saw."

"It don't look like nothin', to me," Alice said. "Not like nothin' I ever saw, even in a circus."

"Did you ever go to a circus?" Dulcie asked the little old man. "Alice has been."

"I don't know," the little old man answered. "It used to seem like I could kind of remember going to one, but that was a long time ago and now I don't know if I remember or not."

"It's in a big tent," George said. "A tent big enough to hold our house. I wish I had a circus tent."

"It has flags on it," Dulcie added, "colored flags flapping on top of it."

"I want to go to a circus," Dicky said.

"We are going to the next one. Mother has already said we could. Alice is going to take us, aren't you, Alice?"

"And a band," added Alice, "and a elefump big as ten of these ponies rolled into one. That elefump was the biggest thing I ever seen in my bawn days. Lawd, Lawd."

"I want to go to a circus, Alice," Dicky said.

"So does I, honey. Spotted hawses, and folks spanglin' through the air . . . listen: don't I hear a band now?"

It was a horn they heard, and they rode on and came to a huge gray castle. The redheaded boy stopped again. "Which way now?" he asked.

"That way," the little old man answered, pointing. A soldier on the wall of the castle was blowing the horn. They rode on and passed the castle, and a little further on they came to a curious tree beside the road. It was a white tree, and at first they thought it was a dogwood tree in bloom. But when they came up to it they saw that the leaves were white.

"What a funny tree," Dulcie said. "What kind of tree is it?"

"It's a—a mellomax tree," the little old man said. "There are a lot of them in this forest."

"I never saw a tree with white leaves before," Dulcie said, and she pulled one of the leaves off, and as soon as she touched it, the leaf changed its color and became a lovely blue. Then they all pulled a leaf off the tree. George's leaf turned purple, and the redheaded boy's was gold; and

Alice took one and hers became bright red, and she held Dicky up and he got one, and his was not any color especially—kind of faint pinks and greens and mostly the same shade of blue as Dulcie's, but paler.

"What color is yours?" Dulcie asked the old man, who showed them his leaf, and it was almost exactly like Dicky's except for the blue.

"That's the color of everybody's wishes," the redheaded boy told them. "Dulcie's are blue, and Dicky's are not very much of anything yet, because he's little, but they'll be blue when he gets bigger, because he is Dulcie's brother; and Alice's are red wishes, and George's are purple, and mine are gold ones; and yours—" to the little old man "—are the same as Dicky's because you don't have many wishes either."

"Why, this may be the Wishing Tree," Dulcie said.

"No, no," the little old man answered. "This is not the Wishing Tree: I've been to the Wish-

ing Tree too many times. This is a mellomax tree."

"Well, which way is the Wishing Tree, then?" the redheaded boy asked.

"That way," the little old man said promptly. And so they rode on.

"It's an awful long way," George said, "and I'm hungry. I wish I had a sandwich." And then George nearly fell off his pony in surprise, for there in his hand was a sandwich. George stared at the sandwich, then he smelled it, then he bit it, and whooped for joy.

"I want something to eat too," Dicky said, and as soon as he said it there was something in his hand.

"What you got in your hand, honey?" Alice asked. The others crowded around the cart to see also.

"What in the world is it?" Dulcie asked. The redheaded boy pinched a bit of it off and put it in his mouth. "What does it taste like?"

"It doesn't taste like anything," the boy said, "because it isn't anything. It's just Something. That was what Dicky said he wanted, you see— he didn't say bread or candy, he just said he wanted Something."

"I want some candy," Dicky said, and immediately it was a cake of chocolate that he held in his hand.

"Alice, you know he can't have candy," Dulcie said.

"That's right, honey," Alice said. "You don't want no old candy, do you?"

"Wants candy," Dicky repeated.

"You better have somethin' else. Here, give me your candy." Alice took the candy out of his hand, but as soon as she did so, the candy disappeared.

Alice sat for a moment in astonishment. Then she whirled upon the little old man.

"You, old man," Alice said, "you give me back that candy, you hear? Taking right out of a baby's hand, like that. You, give me that candy, you hear?"

"Why," the little old man said with surprise, "I didn't take it. You took it yourself."

"Don't you try to prank with me!" Alice exclaimed. "Didn't somebody took it right out of my hand?"

"Why, Alice!" said Dulcie. "He didn't take it."

"Somebody did, then. And he is the closest." Alice glared at the little old man.

"It just went," the redheaded boy explained. "Dicky was the one who wished it, and when Alice took it, it just went, because Alice hadn't wished for candy."

"Well, I don't like no such goin' on around me. I think we better turn around and go home."

"I'm hungry," Dicky said. "I want—"

"Don't you want some bread and butter and sugar?" Dulcie said quickly. "Or cookies?"

"Wants cookies," Dicky said, and as soon as he said it, he had one in each hand.

"Well, if that isn't the funniest thing!" Dulcie exclaimed. "That must have been the Wishing Tree back there."

"No, no," the little old man said, "I know the Wishing Tree too well. That was just a mellomax tree."

"Well, whatever it was, I'm hungry too. Suppose we stop and all wish ourselves something to eat," the redheaded boy suggested. So they stopped and hitched the ponies. "Now, Dulcie, you wish first."

"I want—I want . . . Let me think what I want. Oh, yes: I want some green peas and ladyfingers and an alligator pear and a chocolate malted milk." And as soon as she spoke, there they were on the grass before her.

"Now, Dicky," said the redheaded boy.

"Alice, you'll have to wish for him," Dulcie said. "What do you want, darling?"

"You wants some rice and gravy, don't you, honey?" asked Alice.

"Wants wice and gravy," said Dicky, and there it was before him.

"Now, George," said the redheaded boy.

"I want so much strawberries and chocolate cake that I'll be sick for a week." And immediately there was a huge bowl of strawberries and a fresh chocolate cake before him.

"Now, Alice," said the redheaded boy.

"I wants some ham and gravy and cornbread and a cup of coffee," Alice said, and there it was.

"Now, you choose," the redheaded boy said to the little old man.

"I'll take apple pie and ice cream," the little old man said. "We don't have ice cream very much at home," he explained.

"Now it's my turn," the redheaded boy said. "I want some hot gingerbread and an apple."

They sat on the ground and ate.

"George, you're going to be terribly sick if you eat all that cake and those strawberries," Dulcie said.

"Don't care," George mumbled. "That's what I want."

When they had all finished they got on the

ponies again. The redheaded boy turned to the old man. "Which way now?" he asked.

"That way," the little old man answered, and they went on through the forest.

"I wish I hadn't eaten so much," George said.

"I wish we'd find the Wishing Tree pretty soon. That's what I wish," Dulcie said. A little further on the road forked again.

"That way," the little old man said, and they went on.

"I don't feel good," George said.

"Why, there's that white tree again," Dulcie said with surprise. "We've come back to it."

"No, no," the little old man said. "That's not the same one. That's just another mellomax tree. There's a lot of them in this forest."

"I believe it's the same one, myself," the red-headed boy said.

"So does I," Alice agreed. "I don't believe he knows where that Wishing Tree is no more than we does. Did you ever see that Wishing Tree?"

"I've been to it more than a hundred times," the little old man answered. "I know exactly where it is."

"Have you been to it, really?" asked Dulcie.

"I cross my heart, I have," the little old man said. "I used to go to it every day when I was a young man. Cross my heart and hope to die."

"Well, this certainly looks like the same tree, to me," the redheaded boy said. "Which way, now?"

"Don't youall pay no more mind to him," Alice said. "He don't no more know where that tree is than I does." Alice's voice mumbled on, and Dulcie asked,

"What did you say, Alice?"

"I says, he ain't no better than a old tramp, that's what I says." She turned and glared at the little old man, who cringed back into the corner of the cart.

"If we just had a gun," he said to Dicky, "we could shoot some of these squirrels and birds, couldn't we, now? There's lots of game in this forest."

"I want a gun," Dicky said, and Alice flung up her hands and shrieked, for there was a gun in Dicky's hands, a gun so big that he couldn't hold it and so it dropped right on the little old man's foot.

"You—" said Alice, and she shrieked again. "You, young redheaded man, you take us right back home 'fore this old fool kills us all dead. You come here and get this gun. Look at him, pullin' a gun out on me and this baby!"

"Why, Alice!" exclaimed Dulcie, "he didn't do it! It was Dicky that wished the gun!"

"I don't care who done it. Just look at him there, grinnin' at us, waitin' a chance to rob and kill us all." She turned and glared at the little old man.

"Honest, ma'am," the little old man said, "I never done it. I wouldn't even think—"

"Hush your mouf and get that gun out of

this cart." The little old man stooped and put his hand on the gun, but as soon as he touched it, it disappeared, because he hadn't wished for the gun. "Well," Alice said, "where is it? Take it right out from under your coat, 'fore I calls a policeman."

"Alice," Dulcie exclaimed, "don't you see it's gone? It's gone, Alice. He didn't wish for a gun, it was Dicky who wished for the gun."

Alice flopped around on the seat. "We's goin' right straight home: you tell that redheaded boy to pick out the first road. I'se had about all of this goin' on I can stand." Alice went to mumbling again, and they rode on, and soon they came to the gray castle again. There were some soldiers marching through the gate.

"Look at the soldiers," Dulcie said.

"I don't feel very good," George said. The soldiers marched through the gate, with a flag at the head of the company. Once Alice had a husband who was a corporal in the army. I mean, a

husband that Alice used to have was a soldier
also.

"A soldier's life is awful hard," Alice said.

"I want a soldier," Dicky said.

"You . . ." Alice exclaimed. "Where you
been?"

The soldier that Dicky had wished for touched
his soldier hat. "Why, if it ain't Alice," he said.

"And I'll Alice you," Alice shouted, "if I
jes' had a stick of stovewood in my hand—"
Alice blinked her eyes at the stick of wood, then
she threw it at the soldier, but as soon as it

touched him, it disappeared. "Jes' give me one more stick," and there was another in her hand, and she threw it and it disappeared too. The soldier ducked behind a tree.

"Lawd a mussy, woman," he said. "What is you chunkin' at me? Birds?"

"You triflin' vilyun," said Alice, and she started to climb out of the cart.

"Alice!" exclaimed Dulcie. "What in the world!"

"It's that husban' I used to have. The one that run off on me and lef' me with a month houserent and not even a hunk of sidemeat in the house, and me payin' a lawyer to fin' out what the gov'ment done with him. Him and his army! I'll war him, I will: he ain't never seen no war like what I can aggravoke. You come out from behime that tree."

"Don't you hurt my soldier!" Dicky shouted.

"Run, run," the little old man said. "She ain't got a flatiron or a rollingpin."

"Hol' up," the soldier said. "I can explain how come I never got back."

"I bet you can," Alice retorted. "You come right here and get in this buggy and save your explainin' twell we get home." The soldier came up and got in the cart.

"Don't you hurt my soldier," Dicky repeated.

"He's Alice's soldier, darling," Dulcie said. "Is that the soldier you lost in the war, Alice?"

"He's the one," Alice answered. "And a good losin', too. Look at him! even the war don't want him!"

They drove on. The soldier and the little old man sat side by side at the back of the cart.

"What's your husband's name, Alice?" Dulcie asked.

"Name Exodus," Alice answered. "They was two of 'em. The other one was name Genesis, but meanness kilt him 'fore he was ten years old."

"I was in a war," the little old man said to Alice's husband.

"Which one?" Alice's husband asked.

"I never did know," the little old man answered. "There was a lot of folks in it, I remember."

"Sound like the one I was at," Alice's husband said.

"They're all about alike, I reckon," the little old man said.

"I 'speck you's right," Alice's husband agreed. "Was it across the water?"

"Across the water?" the little old man repeated.

"Across the big up and down water," Alice's husband explained. "Man, man, that was a war. A hundred days, and jes' water, up and down and up and down, and when you looked out you never seen nothin'. Not even sagegrass. I knowed they killed folks in wars, but it seemed like day after day that I jes' couldn't die. I don't know how in the world folks ever dammed up a pond that big. Nor what they can do with it. That water 'ud hol' all the excursion boats in the rentire world."

"No, this wasn't that war. They came right down in my pappy's pasture and fought the war I went to."

"Well, now," said Alice's husband, "if that ain't makin' war comvenient!"

"And there was another war I went to. It was at a place named Seven Pines."

"Were you behind one of them?" Dulcie asked.

"No, ma'am," the little old man answered. "There were more than seven generals in that war."

"Well, now," said Alice's husband, "wars don't change, does they?"

"I don't feel good," George said. "I think . . ." George's eyes had a faraway look in them. "I think I'm going to be sick."

"Who won the war you were in?" Dulcie asked.

"I don't know, ma'am," the little old man answered. "I didn't."

"That's right, too," Alice's husband agreed. "I never seed a soldier yet that ever won anything in a war. But then, whitefolks' wars is always run funny. Next time the whitefolks has a war, I think I ain't goin'. I think I'll jes' stay in the army instead."

"I guess that's better," the little old man agreed.

"I think," said George, "that I'm going to be sick." And George sat right on his pony and got dreadfully sick.

"He sho' did," Alice's husband said. "He couldn't a got no sicker goin' to the far offest war in the whole world."

They all stopped, and presently George got a little better, and they helped him into the cart.

"Can I ride his pony, mister?" the little old man said to the redheaded boy. The redheaded boy said Yes, and the little old man hopped out of the cart and mounted the pony.

"Why didn't you wish for a pony before, if you wanted to ride on one?" Dulcie asked the little old man. "You haven't wished for anything except apple pie and ice cream. Can't you think of something you'd like to wish for?"

"I don't know," the little old man said. "I hadn't thought about it. But I will think of something. Let's see . . . I wish we all had a sack of pink and white striped candy." And as soon as he said it, everyone had a sack of candy in his hand.

"Mine are soft ones," the little old man said. "I used to like the hard ones best, but now I have to eat the soft kind, because my teeth ain't what they used to be when I was a young man."

"Let me see your teeth," Dulcie said, and the little old man opened his mouth. He didn't have any teeth at all.

"Why don't you wish for some false teeth?" Dulcie asked.

"What are false teeth?" asked the little old man.

"Wish for some and see," Dulcie suggested.

"All right. I wish I had some false teeth," the little old man said, and he clapped his hand to his mouth and looked at Dulcie with astonishment.

"Don't you like them?" Dulcie asked.

"I don't really believe I do," the little old man answered. "I've got used to not having any, you see." He took the teeth out and looked at them. "They're right pretty, ain't they? They'd look right nice on the mantelpiece, now, wouldn't they? I think I'll just keep them for that."

They rode on through the forest, under the huge oak trees. There were a lot of birds in these trees, chirping to one another, and squirrels scudded across the grass from one tree to another, and there were flowers of all kinds and colors in the grass.

The little old man kicked his pony with his

heels until it leapt and pranced, and the little bells on the bridle jingled like mad. "We rode horses in that war I used to go to," the little old man said. "This is the way I used to do." And he made the pony dash down the road until the little old man's beard streamed out behind him in the wind, then he made the pony whirl and come dashing back.

"I bet you never went to no war in your life," Alice said.

"I bet so too," George said. George was feeling better now. "I bet if you ever saw a enemy, you'd run."

"I bet I wouldn't," the little old man replied. "I bet I'd cut him right in two with my sword. If I just had a sword in my hand, I'd show you exactly how I'd do." And there was the sword in his hand—a new shiny one, with a gold handle, and the little old man looked at the sword and rubbed it on his coat until it shone like a mirror, and he showed his sword to Alice's husband.

Alice's husband said it was a fine sword, but he said it was a little too long to suit him, because he liked a knife you could hang on a string down your back, inside your shirt.

"This is the way I used to do at the war," the little old man explained. "Watch me." And he waved his sword and made his pony dash down the road again and then come flying back.

"I bet you'd be scared as scared," George said.

"I bet I wouldn't be scared of a hundred enemies," the little old man said. "I bet I'd just ride right into 'em and slice 'em in two with a sword like this."

"I bet you wouldn't slice a dog in two," George said. "I bet you'd be scared."

"I bet I wouldn't," the little old man answered. "I bet I'd just—"

"I bet you'd be scared of a tiger or a lion," George said.

"I bet I've killed a hundred tigers and lions in this very forest," the little old man said,

"with a sword just like this . . . No, I used the sword in the war. I don't remember what I killed the tigers and lions with. It was something else."

"I guess you kilt 'em dodgin' rollin' pins and flatirons," Alice said.

"If I was runnin' a war," Alice's husband said, "I'd get me a bunch of married women and I'd blindfold 'em and I'd p'int 'em and I'd say, 'Go right straight like you's headed and when you hits somethin', it's your husband.' That's the way I'd conduck a war."

"It would save money, wouldn't it?" the little old man said, "because they could pick up the flatirons and rollingpins and throw them again, couldn't they?"

"I've knowed some that don't need no flatirons and rollin' pins," Alice's husband said. "Wait twell you's been married as freqump as I is."

"Yaaah," said George, "I bet if a lion jumped

out from behind a tree in front of you, you'd fall dead."

"I bet I wouldn't," said the little old man, waving his sword again, "I bet I'd just—"

"I wish a lion would ju—"

Dulcie screamed, and George didn't even finish what he was saying, and Alice's husband bellowed like a foghorn, but Alice's voice drowned them all; and they flew down the road. Alice's husband climbed a tree, and Alice ran carrying Dicky in one arm and dragging Dulcie by the other, and behind them came George howling at the top of his voice. But the little old man, still carrying his sword, distanced them all.

"Stop! Stop!" the redheaded boy shouted, and Alice stopped and leaned against a tree, panting for breath. There, in the middle of the road, sat the lion, and near it on his snorting pony was the redheaded boy. "Come back," the redheaded boy called to them, "he won't hurt you."

"Not twell you get that thing out of here," Alice said. "You, Dulcie! Don't you go back up there."

"All you have to do," the redheaded boy said, "is for the one that wished the lion to unwish him. Who was it who wished him? It was George, wasn't it?"

"I guess so," George answered.

"Well, do you want him?" the redheaded boy asked.

"Not me," replied George. "I hope I never see another one." And as soon as George said this, the lion was gone.

"Now we can go back," Dulcie said.

"You, Dulcie!" Alice exclaimed. "Don't you go up there! That thing jes' jumped behime that tree: I seen him!"

"No, no," the redheaded boy said, "he's gone. Come on back."

They went back. Alice had to look behind all the trees, but the lion was really gone.

"Why, where are the ponies?" Dulcie asked.

"Youall wished them away when you saw the lion," the redheaded boy said. "When the lion jumped out, everybody wished he could run, and you can't run while you're sitting on a pony or in a cart."

They all looked at one another in astonishment. "Will we have to walk?" Dulcie asked.

"Well, I haven't got any more ponies in my satchel," the redheaded boy replied.

"I 'speck we better walk," Alice said. "The more we rides, the further we gets from home. They's somethin' mighty cur'us about this," Alice added and she glared at the little old man, who came up with his sword.

"I've lost my gillypus," the little old man said. "It fell out of my pocket, and now I can't find it."

"That's too bad," Dulcie said. "It was a nice gillypus. Don't you wish it could walk and talk, and then you could find it."

"I sure do," the little old man answered. "It was the best gillypus I ever saw." And as soon as he spoke, they heard a scuffling through the grass, and a little thin voice crying,

"Here I come, Egbert; here I come."

"That's my name," the little old man said. The scuffling came nearer, and soon they saw the gillypus running through the grass.

"Little puppy," exclaimed Dicky, and he caught up a stick from the ground and hit the gillypus, and every time he hit it, the gillypus got larger and larger.

"Darling!" exclaimed Dulcie. "Don't hit Egbert's gillypus! Alice! Alice!"

"Kill little puppy," Dicky said. The gillypus was as large as a dog, now. "Cut little puppy in two," Dicky said, and the gillypus fell in two pieces.

"Look what you done!" said the little old man, and he hid his face in his elbow, and wept.

"I'm awful sorry," said Dulcie. "Dicky's a bad boy to cut your gillypus in two."

Then another little voice wailed from the grass at their feet, and they looked down and there was Dicky, no bigger than a lead soldier.

"That's because he made a bad wish," the redheaded boy explained, "a wish that hurt something."

"Don't step on him!" shrieked Dulcie, and almost at the same moment Dulcie and Alice were little like Dicky, and Alice picked Dicky up and held Dulcie against her with the other arm.

"You old fool," Alice shouted up to the little old man in her thin tiny voice. "Look what you done! Don't you step on us!"

"I don't know what to do now," the redheaded boy said. "Dicky'll have to stay little until he does a kind deed for someone, and Dulcie and Alice won't get big again as long as Dicky must stay little."

"I think we all better get little, too," the little old man suggested, "so we can stay together."

"All right," the redheaded boy agreed. "That's the best idea."

"Not me," said George quickly. "I don't want to be that little. I wish I was home." And George just disappeared.

"I'm sorry he's gone," the little old man said. "I could have killed that lion, if I hadn't been so surprised."

Then the others were all little, like Alice and Dulcie and Dicky.

"Gee," said the little old man. They were in a huge forest of the funniest trees. The trees were green all over, and they were flat, like huge sword blades, and they didn't have any branches or leaves at all.

"That's grass," the redheaded boy explained. "We better go this way."

They went on among the funny flat trees, and soon they came to a yellow mountain.

"This is a funny mountain," the little old man said. "It's made out of wood." They walked along beside the mountain, trying to find a road up it. But the mountain went on across the path, and they couldn't get by it.

"I know what it is," the redheaded boy said. "It's Egbert's gillypus."

"I wish I had my gillypus," the little old man said, and they stared in astonishment, for the mountain disappeared, and then the little old man said, "Something jumped in my pocket then." And he put his hand in his pocket and took out his gillypus. "Well," the little old man said, "I'm certainly glad to get this gillypus back again. It's the best gillypus I ever made."

So they went on, and they came out of the forest into a great desert, and standing in the middle of the desert was the biggest beast Alice had ever seen, or Alice's husband either.

"It's bigger'n that elefump," Alice said.

"It's just my pony," the redheaded boy explained. "He knows the way home, all right."

They went on across the desert, and then all of a sudden a jaybird twice as big as an eagle flew down at them. Alice caught Dicky up again and grabbed Dulcie with the other hand, and the jaybird whirled about them, trying to peck Dicky up with his beak. Alice's husband aimed his rifle

and shot at
the jaybird, but
the jaybird kept on
whirling about them, try-
ing to eat Dicky up. The jaybird thought Dicky was a bug, because Dicky was so little.

"Put your hat on the ground!" the redheaded
boy shouted to the little old man, while Alice's
husband was fighting the jaybird, and the little
old man put his hat on the ground and the redheaded boy wished the little old man's hat was
as big as a soup plate, and it was; and they all
got under it. They could hear the jaybird pecking
at the hat, but he couldn't get in.

Finally they couldn't hear the jaybird any more,
and Alice's husband raised the hat and looked
out.

"He's done gone," Alice's husband said. Then
he dropped the hat and jumped back inside.

"Lawd save us," Alice's husband shouted, "here comes a earthquake!"

And all of a sudden the ground rose up beneath them and they tumbled over one another and fell down a big hill, and the hat rolled over, and down they went tumbling, and they could see the earthquake going on past them. They could see the ground hunching up like something was burrowing along under it.

"It's a mole," the redheaded boy said, "that's what it was. Come on, we better get back into the forest and think what to do."

They ran back among the funny flat trees again.

"I think," the redheaded boy said, "that we'd better wish Alice's husband big again, and we'll all get in his hat and he can carry us home."

So they wished Alice's husband big again, and he put his hat on the ground and picked them up one at a time very carefully and put them in the hat.

"You big fool," Alice shouted at him in her tiny high voice, "you pick me and this baby up easy, or I'll tear your head clean off and unravel your backbone down to your belt."

Then Alice's husband picked up his hat and went on. Dulcie and Dicky and Alice and the redheaded boy and the little old man sat in the hat. They couldn't see anything except Alice's husband's head and the sky and the treetops, and after a while Dicky went to sleep, and Dulcie began to get drowsy. But she couldn't get comfortable, because there wasn't a pillow in Alice's husband's hat.

I wish I was in my nice soft bed, Dulcie said to herself. "No I don't! No I don't!" she screamed, but it was too late, for she was again in her bed at home, in her room by herself. "I don't want to be here!" Dulcie wailed. "I want to find Mr. Egbert so he can tell me where the others went!"

And once more she was in front of a gray

cottage with roses growing over the door. "This is not where I left them!" Dulcie said. "I want to be where Alice and Dicky and Maurice and Mr. Egbert and Exodus are." But nothing happened, and Dulcie remembered her colored leaf, and she put her hand in the pocket of her dress. The leaf was gone.

Dulcie didn't know what to do. She stood in the road in front of the cottage, and then she heard somebody chopping wood behind the house, and she opened the gate and entered the front yard. The door of the cottage was closed, and on the ground near the door were some slivers of wood where someone had been whittling with a knife, and scattered about the yard were a flatiron and a rollingpin and an alarm clock. Dulcie went on around the house and there was a little old man with a long gray beard, chopping wood. Dulcie went up to the little old man.

"Where are the others, Mr. Egbert?" Dulcie asked.

The little old man dropped his axe and whirled around. "Ma'am?" the little old man said.

"I've lost them," Dulcie explained. "We were all together there, and now I can't find them," she wailed.

"Was it a picnic?" the little old man asked. "I used to go to a lot of picnics."

"Why, you were with us. Did you get lost, too?" asked Dulcie.

The little old man had the kindest blue eyes. "I used to go to a lot of picnics," the little old man said. "But I ain't been to one now in a long while."

"Why, you were with us this morning!" Dulcie exclaimed with surprise. "Don't you remember? You had apple pie and ice cream!"

"Did I now?" the little old man said. He waggled his long gray beard. "I used to be a great hand for ice cream, in my day. But we don't have ice cream very often, now." The little old man pushed the wood he had been chopping aside.

"Won't you have a seat on this log?" the little old man said politely.

Dulcie sat down sadly. "Then you don't know where they are?" she asked.

The little old man sat down also. "Lordy, Lordy," he said, "it's been a power of years since I went to a picnic. But then, I ain't as young as I once was, and I've kind of got lazy. That's the reason I chop wood, you see, for a little exercise."

"How old are you?" Dulcie asked.

"I'm ninetytwo this past gone April a year," the little old man replied.

"And so you don't know where they are," Dulcie said. "I was with them, and then I got l-lost, and now I c-can't f-find them, and I'm sc-scared," Dulcie wept.

The little old man jumped up nervously, and he made a clicking sound with his tongue. Suddenly he reached into his pocket. "Look what I made," he said.

Dulcie wiped her eyes and looked. "Why, it's the gillypus!" she exclaimed.

"Is that what it is?" the little old man said, pleased. "I didn't know what it was. You can have it, if you want," he added.

"I want Alice and Dicky," Dulcie said, weeping again.

The little old man clicked his tongue and put his hands in his pockets again. "Look here what I found in the road this morning. I thought at first it was a leaf, but now I believe it's a dragon's scale or a roc's feather."

Dulcie looked at the leaf and clapped her hands. While the old man held it, it was not any color especially, just a faint pinkish greenish color. "You can have it, if you want," the little old man said.

"Oh, thank you, thank you!" Dulcie exclaimed, grasping the leaf tight in her palm. "If we go on another picnic soon, we'll come for you," Dulcie promised. "Thank you, thank you!"

"I used to be a great hand for picnics," the little old man said, and then his wife opened the kitchen door.

"You, Egbert!" she shouted, and slammed the door again. The little old man caught up the axe and chopped wood furiously.

"Now," said Dulcie, clasping her blue leaf tightly in her hand and shutting her eyes, "I want to be where Dicky and Alice and Maurice and Exodus—"

"Hello, Dulcie, hello, Dulcie!" they all cried, and Dulcie hugged Dicky and Alice, and Alice and Dicky hugged Dulcie, and Alice's husband gashed his mouth from ear to ear until all his teeth showed, and the redheaded boy watched them with his queer yellowflecked eyes.

"How did Dicky get big again?" Dulcie asked.

"That old tramp los' his gillymus in one of the wrinkles in Exodus' hat, and Dicky foun' it for him," Alice explained. And Dulcie hugged

Dicky and Alice again, and Alice and Dicky hugged Dulcie again.

"Come on," the redheaded boy said. They were in a valley now, and pretty soon they would reach a river. The valley was full of sweet odors, and they walked on and soon they saw a tree covered with leaves of a thousand different colors.

"It's the Wishing Tree!" Dulcie exclaimed.

"I guess that's what it is," the redheaded boy agreed, but when they got close to the tree the leaves flew up into the air and whirled about the tree, and then they saw that the tree was a tall old man with a long shining beard like silver, and the leaves were birds of all colors and kinds.

"Good morning, Father Francis," the redheaded boy said.

"Good morning, Maurice," the good Saint Francis replied, and the colored birds whirled and sang about him, lighting on his shoulders and head and arms.

"This is Dulcie, and Dicky, and Alice and Alice's husband," the redheaded boy said.

"We are looking for the Wishing Tree," Dulcie explained.

The good Saint Francis looked at them and his eyes twinkled. "And did you find it?"

"We don't know," Dulcie replied. "We thought perhaps this is it."

The good Saint Francis thought a while, and the birds settled about him like a colored cloud. Then he spoke, and the birds whirled again into the air and spun around his head.

"Didn't you each pick a leaf from a tree back there in the forest?" the good Saint Francis asked.

"Yes, Father Francis," Dulcie said.

"Well, that was the Wishing Tree. But suppose there had been a thousand leaves on it, and a thousand boys and girls had each taken one, when the next one came along, there wouldn't be any leaf for him, would there?"

"No, Father Francis," Dulcie said.

"So a wish you make that way is a selfish wish, isn't it?"

"Yes, Father Francis."

"Then," the good Saint Francis said, "give me your leaves so I can put them back, and instead I'll give you each one of my birds. And if you'll feed it and care for it, you'll never make a selfish wish, because people who care for and protect helpless things cannot have selfish wishes. Will you do this?"

"Yes, Father Francis," they all answered. So they gave the good Saint Francis their leaves, and in exchange he took from beneath his gown a wicker cage and he put a bluebird in it for Dulcie, and he took another cage and put an oriole in it for the redheaded boy, and he gave Alice a redbird, and to Dicky a little white bird with pale blue feathertips, because he was little and because he was Dulcie's brother.

"What about Alice's husband?" Dulcie asked.

"He will help Alice feed her redbird," the

good Saint Francis replied. "Because if he leaves her again, he'll only be a selfish wisher."

"And George?" Dulcie asked.

"Wishing is not good for George," the good Saint Francis replied. "The first wish he made, he was punished for, the second wish he made, he frightened you all for no reason whatever, and the third wish he made, he deserted you while you were in trouble."

"But Mr. Egbert," Dulcie said. "He deserves one, doesn't he?"

"Ah," answered the good Saint Francis, "he already has more than I can give him: he is old, and he no longer has any wishes at all. What became of him, by the way?"

"His wife come and got him," Alice answered.

"Then," the good Saint Francis said, "he doesn't even need anything else."

He ceased to speak and the birds settled down again about his head and shoulders.

"Goodbye, Father Francis," they said. "And

thank you." But the good Saint Francis only smiled at them from amid his birds, and they went on.

They came to the bank of the river. But the funniest thing was, it wasn't a flat river, but it stood up on its edge, like a gray wall.

"If that isn't the funniest thing!" Dulcie said, because the river was like the mist had been, and in it they could see a dim thing like a street stretching on between houses, straight in front of them, and the water smelled like wistaria.

"We'll have to go through it," the redheaded boy said.

"Oh, I'm afraid to," Dulcie said. "Wait." But the redheaded boy had already stepped into it, and Alice and Dicky and Alice's husband followed him. "Wait!" called Dulcie again, but they were only dim shapes, and the redheaded boy turned his thin ugly face and his queer goldflecked eyes, while his hair made a little glow about him, and beckoned to her. "Wait,"

called Dulcie again, and she stepped into the
mist too, and felt with her hands before her.
But the others had disappeared ahead of her, and
she could see only the faint glow of the redheaded
boy's hair in the mist, and it was like she was in
a round bowl of sleep, rising and rising through
the warm waters of sleep, to the top. And then
she would be awake.

And she was awake, and it was like there was

another little balloon inside her, getting bigger and bigger, making her body and arms and legs tingle as though she had just eaten a piece of peppermint. What is it? she thought. What can it be?

"Birthday, birthday!" cried a voice near her, and her eyes flew open and there was Dicky jumping up and down on the bed beside her, and leaning over her was her mother. Dulcie's mother was beautiful, so slim and tall, with her grave unhappy eyes changeable as seawater and her slender hands that came so softly about you when you were sick.

"Look," her mother said, and she held out a wicker cage with a bluebird in it, and Dulcie squealed with delight.

"I wants a bird, mamma," Dicky said, "I wants a bird, mamma."

"You can have half of mine, darling," Dulcie said, and she let Dicky hold the cage, and she closed her eyes again and her mother's hand came on her forehead, and Dulcie remembered the good Saint Francis, and Maurice, with his queer eyes and his flaming hair. Well, she had her bluebird, even if it had been just a dream, and the good Saint Francis had said that if you are kind to helpless things, you don't need a Wishing Tree to make things come true. And next year she would have another birthday, and if she just remembered to get into bed left foot first and to turn the pillow over before she went to sleep, who knows what might happen?

Publisher's Note

Until the appearance of this edition, only a single copy of this book existed. It is a small book (5¼ x 6¾ inches), typed and bound by the author in varicolored paper. On the left-hand page facing the dedicatory verse is typed:

single mss. impression
oxford-mississippi-
5-february-1927

There is another slightly longer version of the story, apparently an earlier draft, and several typed copies of it exist. This Random House edition follows the unique copy, which the author completed almost a year after the publication of his first novel, and just before the appearance of his second. Where the spellings of dialect speech are not consistent within the typed book, they have been edited in favor of the simpler or normal spellings—a process that undoubtedly would have been much extended by the author, as was his practice in later works, if he had been present to prepare the script for 1967 publication.

Set in Monotype Centaur,
a type face designed by Bruce Rogers,
by Westcott & Thomson, Inc., Philadelphia, Pennsylvania
Printed on Curtis Tweedweave Ivory by Halliday
Lithograph Corporation, West Hanover, Massachusetts
Bound in Bancroft Lynnene by The Book Press
Incorporated, Brattleboro, Vermont
Designed by Betty Anderson